Written by Loredana Cunti
Illustrated by Stacy Curtis

Kids Can Press

Kakapo was crazy about karate.

From the time she was a Kinder Kakapo, she had been interested in the martial arts: kung fu, judo, tae kwon do.

But karate was her favorite. She loved the blocks, the strikes, the stances — and she especially loved the superfast kicks:

the side kicks …

the jumping kicks …

the running kicks …

… and the flying kicks.

Well, maybe not the flying kicks.
(Fact: kakapos can't fly.)

Kakapo knew what it took to master karate — time and hard work. And she was committed. Every day, she went to the dojo to practice with the other students.

Some days, she focused on her blocks.

Low block

High block

Rising block

Other days, she concentrated on her strikes.

Tomorrow was a big day for Kakapo. It was Belt Test Day at the dojo.

She was excited — and she was ready! But just in case, she practiced her stances one last time before bed.

Half-moon stance

Crane stance

As Kakapo tried to fall asleep, she thought of her previous belt tests.
That perfect block when she got her yellow belt.
Breaking that wooden board when she got her green belt.

That swift side kick when she got her blue belt.
Her sparring footwork when she got her red belt.

But tomorrow would be Kakapo's greatest test. She was trying for her black belt, the most difficult belt of all.

She had no reason to be nervous. She had practiced as much as any bird could and had mastered all the moves.

Except that one ...

But surely the senseis wouldn't ask her to do that?

Kakapo fell asleep hoping the senseis would remember the fact that kakapos can't fly.

The next day, the dojo was filled with nervous birds taking tests. Kakapo straightened her karate gi and waited patiently for her name to be called, all the while trying not to worry.

She spread her wings wide and flapped them, hoping that the senseis would notice and be reminded that she could not actually lift off.

Finally, her turn came.

Kakapo bowed in front of the panel of senseis.

She waited.

"Please start with a running front kick," said the first sensei.

She did the kick — and it was perfect.

"You may proceed to a jumping back kick," said the second sensei.

Kakapo jumped higher than she ever had before.

"Now, you may show us your side snap kick."

She did it. It was flawless.

It continued like that all the way through the test.

Kakapo was on her way to a black belt!

Then, it happened.

"Please show us your flying side kick," said the third sensei.

"My flying side kick?" replied Kakapo.

"Yes," said the sensei.

"You mean, the one with both feet in the air at the same time?" asked Kakapo.

"Yes, the flying side kick."

Kakapo began to explain.

"Ummm, excuse me, Sensei. The thing is … well, the fact is … kakapos can't fly."

The sensei was silent.

"Soooo, since I'm a kakapo, I'm not going to be able to do a flying kick."

The sensei was still silent.

It looked like Kakapo would not be getting her black belt after all.

At last, the sensei spoke. "For your final test of skill, please show us a running, jumping side kick."

A running, jumping side kick? Kakapo didn't know that kick. She had never even heard of it!

Unsure what to do, she thought about all the practice and hard work she had put in for this day. And then she made up her mind: she had to try.

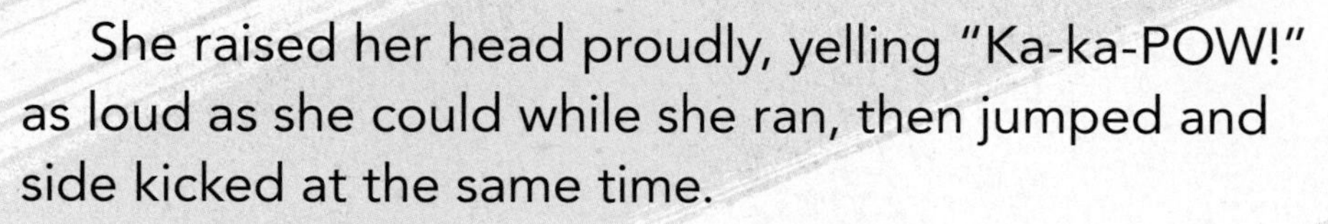

She raised her head proudly, yelling "Ka-ka-POW!" as loud as she could while she ran, then jumped and side kicked at the same time.

She landed in a perfect ready stance.

"Wait," she said to the senseis. "Did I just do a flying side kick?"

The senseis were silent. And then they all smiled.

POW!

Kakapo stepped forward, stretching her wings out to receive her black belt. The other students flapped and clapped, chanting “Ka-ka-POW! Ka-ka-POW!”

“Well done … Karate Kakapo,” said the sensei, bowing deeply.

And Karate Kakapo bowed back.

To Vienna and Maria and all the sporty girls in the world. And to Frederick, for always asking me to play. — L.C.

For Rayna — S.C.

Karate terms used in this book

dojo (*doh-joh*): a school where karate is taught

gi (*gee*): a loose-fitting garment worn by karate students

sensei (*sen-say*): a karate teacher

Kids Can Press gratefully acknowledges the financial support of the Government of Ontario, through the Ontario Media Development Corporation; the Ontario Arts Council; the Canada Council for the Arts; and the Government of Canada for our publishing activity.

Published in Canada and the U.S. by Kids Can Press Ltd.
25 Dockside Drive, Toronto, ON M5A 0B5

Kids Can Press is a Corus Entertainment Inc. company

www.kidscanpress.com

The illustrations were created in pen and ink and watercolor.
The text is set in Avenir.

Edited by Jennifer Stokes
Designed by Julia Naimska

Printed and bound in Malaysia, in 10/2018 by Tien Wah Press (Pte) Ltd.

CM 19 0 9 8 7 6 5 4 3 2 1

Library and Archives Canada Cataloguing in Publication

Cunti, Loredana, 1968–, author
Karate Kakapo / written by Loredana Cunti ; illustrated by Stacy Curtis.

ISBN 978-1-77138-803-0 (hardcover)

I. Curtis, Stacy, illustrator II. Title.

PS8605.U58K37 2019 jC813'.6 C2017-906701-X